P9-DWI-072

The Boxcar Children Mysteries

THE SUMMER CAMP MYSTERY

created by
GERTRUDE CHANDLER WARNER

Illustrated by Hodges Soileau

Albert Whitman & Company
Chicago, Illinois

Contents

THE SUMMER CAMP MYSTERY

CHAPTER 1

Shapes in the Fog

At five o'clock on an August morning, the sun hadn't risen yet, but the Alden family was already up and about. The streetlamps were still on. In a few minutes, the headlights on James Alden's car were on, too.

Four sleepy children trooped down the porch steps of the big white house where they lived. They joined their grandfather, who was already in the car.

"Buckle up, everyone," Grandfather Alden said. "We want to get an early start driving to Maine."

One by one, Henry, Jessie, Violet, and six-year-old Benny Alden slipped into Grandfather's car. They buckled themselves in.

Mr. Alden backed out slowly. He didn't want to scrape the bottom of his car. It was riding low, loaded down with camp trunks, backpacks, and the five Aldens.

The family housekeeper, Mrs. McGregor, stood by the driveway holding on to Watch, the family dog. "Good-bye, children," Mrs. McGregor said. "Have fun at Camp Seagull. Don't eat too much lobster!"

Twelve-year-old Jessie tried not to yawn. She'd barely had time to braid her long brown hair and find her Junior Counselor cap. "Good-bye, Mrs. McGregor. Take good care of Watch for me."

" 'Bye, Mrs. McGregor," the other three children said.

Watch looked at the car with his saddest face. He whined softly, the way he always did when he was left behind.

"Watch wants to come to Camp Seagull with us, too," Jessie said with a little catch in her voice. "I'm going to miss having him sleep at the foot of my bed."

Benny took one last look at Watch and Mrs. McGregor before Mr. Alden pulled away. "Too bad Watch can't be a camper, too. Remember how he found us in our boxcar in the woods — even before you found us, Grandfather?"

Mr. Alden smiled. Benny was quite a chatterbox, even at five o'clock in the morning. "You won't need Watch for company, Benny. The camp is filled with children your age."

"Jessie and I will be right there as Junior Counselors," fourteen-year-old Henry told Benny. "Violet is a camper, too."

"Don't forget," Grandfather Alden said to Benny, "at the end of each day at camp, you'll be joining me at the Dark Harbor Inn."

Violet, who was ten, thought about this. "But the rest of us will be away for the whole week since we're overnight campers.

I'm going to miss you, Grandfather."

"And I'll miss you," Mr. Alden said in a quiet voice. "While I catch up on my reading, you can catch up on your painting and your crafts."

Violet's eyes brightened. "I'm going to spend as much time as I can in the art studio at camp."

Jessie was bubbling with plans. "I'm so glad Ginny and Rich Gullen found room for us in this session of Camp Seagull, Grandfather. There's so much going on. Last night, I looked over the counselor manual again. There's waterskiing, Costume Night, swimming, storytelling, arts and crafts, sports — you name it."

"Eating. You forgot to say eating," Benny said.

Everyone in the car laughed. Who else in the Alden family would be thinking about food so early in the morning?

"Don't worry, Benny, you won't go hungry," Henry said.

"I know. I never go hungry. See?" Benny pulled a bag from the backpack at his feet.

"Mrs. McGregor said it was a long way to Maine. I wanted to be ready, so I packed some trail mix."

"But Benny, we're not going on any trails today," Henry pointed out. "Not until we get out to Claw Island, where Camp Seagull is. You don't need trail mix riding in a car."

Benny disagreed. "Trail mix is good anytime, even on long car rides." He took out some sunflower seeds to munch on. "Especially on long car rides."

Just as the sun came up, Mr. Alden turned onto the busy highway going north. "Off we go, children!"

"Good-bye, Greenfield," Violet said. "See you next week."

By the time Mr. Alden drove into northern Maine, the gas tank was nearly empty. As for the picnic basket Mrs. McGregor had sent along, that was nearly empty, too. And so was Benny's trail mix bag.

Mr. Alden shifted in his seat. He'd been driving a long time. "We're practically there, children. Now that we're off the main highway, let's look for road signs. There's some fog rolling in. I don't want to miss the turnoff for the Claw Island ferry. It's just outside Dark Harbor. I went there all the time when I was a boy."

"Now Henry and I are the boys!" Benny said proudly. "And we're visiting Claw Island just like you did."

"Right you are." Grandfather smiled to himself. "Only there wasn't a camp on the island back then, just the old Pines estate that the family owned, along with some deserted buildings. Many a time my chums and I would go out to Claw Island to explore and play games."

"Just like us — if we ever get there." Benny pressed his forehead against the window.

Violet stared out, too. "The fog has swallowed up everything except for the pointy pine trees."

"Look! There's a sign!" Benny made a claw with his hand. "Why is it called Claw Island, anyway?"

"If you look at a map, you can see the island is shaped like a lobster claw," Jessie explained.

Mr. Alden turned onto a sandy beach road. "And so it was in my grandmother's day. Only back then it was called Claw Point, not Claw Island. It was still connected to the mainland just outside Dark Harbor. One summer, Grandmother returned to discover the ocean had washed away the road. Two hurricanes later, the ocean covered over the beach and the dunes in between."

Jessie flipped through the Camp Seagull manual. "It says here that after the second hurricane, the Pines family turned their property into a camp. Then last winter they sold it to Rich and Ginny Gullen, the new owners."

Mr. Alden drove slowly down the dirt road. "I hope the Gullens make a go of it. Rich told me the Pines family found it difficult running a camp on the island. They had to sell it because they lost too much money. As you can see, it's not an easy place to get to. It can only be reached by boat. People travel out on the small passenger ferry. Camp supplies go on the freight boat once a week."

"We're on the people boat," Benny said. "I just hope the food boat doesn't get lost."

Grandfather smiled. "That's not likely to happen. It's only a ten-minute boat ride from here. Too bad it's foggy right now. On a sunny day, Claw Island is a very pretty sight."

"But not today," Violet said. "There's no sign of the island, just dark shapes and fog everywhere."

Grandfather Alden brought the car to a stop in a small parking area. "Here's the ferry landing, just where it used to be. I see a few other camp families have already arrived."

The Aldens scrambled from the car. They needed to stretch their legs after their long trip. They followed the sound of the lapping ocean right down to a small beach and an empty dock.

The children looked out at the gray water. A few seagulls bobbed in the cove, ducking under now and then for a fish. Everything else was wrapped in fog and strangely silent.

The Aldens returned to the parking area. They looked shyly at the other families milling around in the mist. Some of the children already had on their Camp Seagull shirts. Most of the younger children stayed close to their families, just as Benny and Violet stayed next to Grandfather Alden. Everyone would be saying good-bye soon enough.

CHAPTER 2

Screams on the Beach

Henry and Jessie helped unload Grandfather's car. They carried their trunks toward the dock, where other campers were lining up their luggage.

Jessie smiled at a sandy-haired girl with a ponytail and a Junior Counselor cap. "Hi," she said.

The girl kept on counting the bags and trunks. She didn't seem to hear Jessie.

Jessie greeted the girl again. "I'm Jessie Alden. That's my brother Henry over there. He's also a Junior Counselor. We can help you carry the baggage onto the dock if you'd like."

The girl picked up a heavy duffel bag. "You have to have special counselor training first before you can do certain things. Leave your camp trunks on the beach. I'll put them on the ferry." With that, the girl turned back to her work.

Jessie returned to the other Aldens. "I must have said the wrong thing to that Junior Counselor. I'll wait to ask her what to do when she's not so busy."

Raaaangh!

Several children screamed. Even the grown-ups jumped at the earsplitting sound. Everyone looked around. There was nothing to be seen through the fog.

"Ha! You lose points already," someone nearby said, then cackled. "No screaming at the horn."

Benny stood by Jessie. "Who said that? What are they talking about? It's so foggy, I can't tell what's going on."

Jessie gave Benny a friendly squeeze. "I think they're talking about the No Screaming Medal. It's part of the Camp Seagull Olympics. Campers try to win points for being brave, or neat, or helpful—or quiet."

Henry explained, "The No Screaming Medal goes to the group that has the fewest screamers. There are all kinds of other awards, too. There's a No Food on the Floor Award for the group that drops the least food in the dining hall."

"They give awards for things like that?" Benny asked. "That's easy. I just hope they don't have a No Talking Medal."

Raaaangh! The horn sounded again, even louder.

Everyone jumped. But no one screamed this time.

Where was that terrible sound coming from? The Aldens stared out at the water. A boat, more like a large raft with a railing and a bench all around, chugged toward the shore. At the wheel, an unsmiling man in a pilot's cap looked over the side of the boat to line it up with the dock.

Onboard sat two children, both with curly dark hair. The boy looked about

Jessie's age. The girl seemed to be a few years younger, about nine years old. Both children stared back at the campers on the beach without smiling.

One of the nearby campers whispered to the Aldens, "The boatman is named Booth Pines. But all the campers call him Boo. He shows up in different places to fix things, and you don't know he's there."

The Aldens looked at one another. Camp Seagull seemed a little spookier than they had expected from the camp photographs they had seen.

Benny tapped Grandfather's arm. "Is that the people ferry?"

Mr. Alden smiled. "You can call it that. It's such a short distance to Claw Island, you could almost float over there on a log."

Everyone jumped back when Mr. Pines threw out a heavy rope. Henry grabbed the rope to tie it to the dock.

"Leave that!" the man yelled.

Henry dropped the rope. "Sorry. Just trying to help."

Mr. Pines turned off the ferry engine

then stepped down. "You can help by standing back. Can't have a bunch of strange kids bringing in the boat. There could be some big problems if the ferry floated away."

"Oh, I know lots of sailor knots," Henry explained. "But I don't want to get in your way."

Mr. Pines turned to the boy on the ferry. "Zach, go tie that rope good and tight."

The boy stepped down on the dock. "Sure thing, Dad." The boy, tall like his father, wound the rope around the dock piling.

"Now go help Kim bring up the luggage," the man told his son before turning to the girl. "Lizzie, stay onboard. Zach and Kim will bring up the trunks and duffel bags. Push them under the seats so the weight's even all around."

Zach joined the Junior Counselor who had been collecting the campers' trunks. Together, they began to load the luggage onto the ferry.

The Aldens wanted to help, but they held back. They didn't want the man to scold them the way he had yelled at Henry.

Mr. Alden stepped forward. He studied the man's face before speaking. "Glad to meet you, sir. I'm James Alden. My grandchildren will be staying at Camp Seagull. We'd be glad to lend a hand."

The boatman stared at Mr. Alden for a few seconds. "My children, Zach and Lizzie, are stronger than they look. They know more than anyone here about what needs to be done."

The Aldens stepped away. They found a nearby dune to sit on while they waited for the ferry to be ready.

A few minutes later, a van pulled up. The door opened. A short-haired woman with a big smile stepped out of the van, holding a clipboard. "Mr. Alden!" the woman said. She put out her hand. "Ginny Gullen. Remember me? Of course, I was Ginny Shore way back when I worked at the Dark Harbor Inn. You visited every summer. I remember how you enjoyed having your morning coffee on the porch."

Mr. Alden broke into a big smile. "Virginia Shore! My, my, you're all grown up now. It took a few minutes to connect the face with the name. I've spoken on the phone with your husband, Rich, to make the arrangements for my grandchildren. They're so happy you were able to find spots for them in camp at the last minute."

The Aldens noticed that Mr. Pines and his children frowned when Grandfather said this.

Ginny turned to the Alden children. "Let me guess. Henry, Jessie, Violet. And you're Benny, right?"

"Right," Benny said proudly.

Ginny waved over Zach Pines. He put down the duffel bags he was carrying. "Come meet the Aldens, Zach," Ginny said. "Here are Henry, Jessie, Violet, and Benny. Everybody, meet Zach Pines. His father, Booth, is our ferry pilot and our all-around groundskeeper and assistant. Zach's sister, Lizzie, is also a camper. They live in Dark Harbor now, but they practically grew up on Claw Island. These two know Camp Seagull inside and out."

The Aldens crowded around Zach Pines like a flock of birds. When they noticed Zach seemed shy because of all the attention, they stepped back a little.

Ginny smoothed things over in her cheery way. "Thanks to you, Henry, Zach won't have to run the Flag Ceremony twice a day. He's been doing that since before Rich and I took over," Ginny informed the Aldens. "Now he doesn't have to rush in the morning and after dinner."

"Ginny asked me to pack my bugle," Henry proudly told Zach. "I learned to play it for flag raising in the Scouts."

Zach didn't say anything. He looked as if he wanted to escape the five pairs of eyes fixed on him. "My father needs me now," Zach said before sprinting off to the dock.

"I don't know what Rich and I would do without the Pines family," Ginny said. "I do want Zach and Lizzie to enjoy camp as much as the other campers. Booth is a good father, but he's very serious. He sometimes forgets to let the children relax and have fun." She turned to Henry and Jessie. "I've

assigned some of Zach and Lizzie's respon-
sibilities to both of you. I'd like them to
have some more free time to take part in
camp activities."

"Are they overnight campers?" Jessie
asked.

Ginny frowned. "I'm afraid not. Rich and
I didn't have any more cabin spaces for
overnight campers. Zach and Lizzie are day
campers. Still, I want them to have a great
time, just like everyone else. I'm dividing up
some of the chores Booth has given them
and assigning them to Junior Counselors
like yourselves. In fact, you can go help
them load the ferry right now."

Henry and Jessie stared at each other.

"Ummm . . . we tried to help," Henry
said, "but Mr. Pines said he didn't want any
new kids slowing things up."

"The other Junior Counselor who's helping out said we have to have special training first," Jessie added.

Ginny's smile froze for a second. "Oh,
dear. Let me speak to Booth. He's used to
doing things his way. I suppose he didn't

want any new campers underfoot yet. But your grandfather told my husband what careful, hard workers you are. As for Kim Waters, I sent her over from camp to greet the new campers. I better straighten things out now that I'm here."

The Aldens overheard Ginny talking to Mr. Pines. "Booth, I have two strong helpers here — Henry and Jessie Alden," she said to the boatman.

Kim came over to Ginny. "Hi, Ginny. We still have some more trunks and duffels to get on the ferry."

Ginny had a different idea. "Kim, loading bags isn't what I had in mind for you. I sent you over to welcome the new campers and make them feel at home. I'd like the Aldens to meet you. This is Kim Waters. Kim, meet Mr. Alden and his grandchildren Henry, Jessie, Violet, and Benny. Henry and Jessie are Junior Counselors like you. Violet's one of our overnight campers. And Benny is a day camper."

The girl nodded but didn't say anything even after the Aldens said hello. Instead she turned to Ginny. "I have to finish helping Boo — I mean, Mr. Pines. I know where everything goes," the girl said. "The new campers are still with their families."

"Please attend to the campers," Ginny reminded Kim.

Finally, Kim took a whistle from her pocket and blew it. "Campers, over here! The ferry's about to leave. Let's move it!"

Ginny sighed. "Gentle with the new campers, Kim. They're nervous about leaving their families. You know what? Finish loading the luggage after all. The Aldens can help board the campers."

"Fine with me. That's what I wanted to do anyway," Kim said before heading to the ferry.

Henry and Jessie rounded up the campers. They led them to the boat, talking to them gently so they would look forward to their ferry trip to camp.

"Greetings, Seagulls!" Ginny began, smiling at the children gathered near the dock. "Welcome to Camp Seagull. I'm Ginny Gullen. I'm so glad to meet you at last. We have three Junior Counselors here: Henry and Jessie Alden — and that's Kim Waters over there. Kim is a fifth-year Seagull camper. Now she's a Junior Counselor, too. She'll make sure your luggage gets on board safe and sound."

Henry and Jessie stood aside as the new and old campers said good-bye to their families.

Ginny checked off the children's names. "Mr. Pines is our ferry pilot. He'll bring us out to the island. When we arrive, we'll all gather by the flagpole in front of Evergreen Lodge. Parents and grandparents, please meet your day campers at seven-thirty tonight right here. That's when the ferry brings them back after Flag Ceremony. Now it's time for good-bye hugs, everyone!"

Mr. Alden put his hand on Benny's shoulder. "I'll be right by the dock when the ferry comes in this evening, Benny."

Grandfather turned to Violet. "Enjoy your stay. If you think of your lonesome grandfather when you're in arts and crafts,

I could use another leather change purse or a new coffee mug."

Violet hugged Grandfather. "I'll make you something special."

"And keep an eye on Henry and Jessie," Grandfather told Violet and Benny. "Make sure they have fun. Being Junior Counselors isn't all work."

"You know us, Grandfather," Henry said. "Work is fun for us."

The four Aldens were the last campers to board. " 'Bye, Grandfather," they called out.

Raaaangh! the horn screamed. The ferry pulled away from the dock.

Everyone turned to wave to the families onshore.

That's when Jessie spotted something on the beach that wasn't supposed to be there. She turned to Henry. "Look!" she whispered. "Our trunks are still on the beach — off to the side. See? Kim told me she'd take care of them."

Henry smacked his forehead. "Oh, no!"

Jessie rolled her eyes. "Let's not bother Ginny right now," she whispered. "She's busy. After all, we're Junior Counselors. We're supposed to know better."

"When we get to camp, I'll ask Ginny if Mr. Pines can safely store our trunks tonight when he drops off the day campers," Jessie said. "Maybe he can bring them out in the morning."

This was too much for Kim Waters, who overheard Jessie. "This is the first day of camp," she said. "The Gullens and Boo have a lot of jobs at the camp. They don't have time to make special trips to Dark Harbor all because people leave their things behind."

"But when I wanted to help with the trunks, you told me . . ." Jessie stopped. "Never mind. We'll be more careful next time."

When the Aldens looked back at the beach, the fog had swallowed it up along with their three camp trunks.

CHAPTER 3

Monster Rock

Just as Booth Pines guided the passenger ferry across the water, the fog lifted. Grandfather Alden had been right. Up ahead, a very pretty sight appeared: Claw Island sparkled in the water.

From the boat, the Aldens could see cozy wooden buildings tucked into groves of tall pine trees. A flagpole rose above the large main building.

Jessie grabbed Henry's arm. "The island is so close. I wonder if we could swim between Dark Harbor and Claw Island. After all, we just passed our lifesaving test at the Greenfield Pool."

"You're not allowed," Zach Pines told Jessie. "There are strong currents between the island and Dark Harbor. You could get sucked out to sea."

When some of the younger children heard this, they moved closer to Henry and Jessie.

"Oh, I was just wondering, that's all," Jessie said. She turned to some of the younger children. "My counselor manual said the swimming lessons are given on the bay side of the island. The water is warm and calm there—like a lake."

"Look, a whale!" Benny cried. He pointed to something wide, smooth, and gray off in the water not too far from Claw Island.

The campers swiveled around to see the whale.

"That's Monster Rock, not a whale," Lizzie Pines informed Benny. "When it gets dark, the rock can turn into a monster that comes out of the water. Sometimes we even find giant footprints in the sand."

"Goodness, this isn't the time for that old made-up tale, Lizzie!" Ginny said when she noticed the worried looks of some of the new campers. "Actually, children, that's Seal Rock. Often, if the sun is out and the tide is low, seals climb onto the rock to sun themselves."

With the fog and Monster Rock behind them and Camp Seagull in front of them, the campers had a hard time sitting still. Camp was about to begin!

Onshore, a circle of campers who had arrived earlier stood around the flagpole. Behind them a group of teenagers and young adults waved their Senior and Junior Counselor caps at everyone on the ferry.

"Welcome, Seagulls!" the flagpole crowd yelled out. "Give us a seagull squawk!"

The new campers weren't sure what to do.

"Go ahead," Ginny urged everyone.

"Crawk! Crawk!" the campers screamed out like a flock of seagulls about to land on Claw Island.

"The camp is so pretty," Violet said when

she stepped onto the dock. "Evergreen Lodge looks just the way I pictured — with porches and big windows looking out on the bay."

"You know," Benny said, "Claw Island doesn't look a bit like a scary lobster claw."

"That's only on a map, Benny," Violet said, laughing. "Or if you're a bird looking down."

Ginny waved the campers toward the flagpole group. "There's my husband, Rich."

Rich and Ginny Gullen wore identical CAMP SEAGULL DIRECTOR shirts and nearly identical friendly smiles.

"Greetings," Rich began. "Welcome to Camp Seagull. Hope you had a smooth ride over. Ginny and I are happy to welcome you to our first season as directors of Camp Seagull. The camp has been around since Ginny and I grew up in Dark Harbor. Both of us worked here when we weren't much older than most of you."

Ginny looked around at the campers. "I know some of your parents were once campers here. We've kept up many of the traditions the Pines family started in the past. And we've added a few of our own."

The Aldens noticed Mr. Pines and his children didn't seem in a hurry to join the group.

"Is Mr. Pines related to the family that owned the camp?" Jessie asked Kim in a whisper.

"Yes," Kim whispered back. "But he doesn't mention it. His family had to give up the camp. Now he has to work for Rich and Ginny. They changed everything from before."

"Do you still have Dress Your Favorite Fruit Night?" a girl camper asked Rich.

Rich grinned. "At Camp Seagull we even dress up vegetables! Our campers last session voted to have a Dress Your Favorite Vegetable Night. We've added new activities like that. But it's still the same special place it's always been. Now Ginny will tell you all about the Camp Seagull Olympics."

"Okay, campers. Let's start by lining up," Ginny began. She picked up a big blue bowl. "Come and choose a surprise from this bowl."

Benny tried to peek over the rim of the bowl. "Is it a snack?"

Ginny held the bowl out for Benny. "You'll see."

Benny reached in. "It's a little dolphin." He showed Violet the small plastic animal.

"I picked a seal," she said.

"I got a dolphin," Jessie said after her turn. "So did Henry."

When the bowl was empty, Ginny looked around at all the campers. "During your stay, you'll either be on a dolphin or a seal team, depending on the animal you chose. Half our cabins are Dolphin cabins, and half are Seal cabins. Even day campers have a cabin to spend time in during the day. As for you overnight campers, after our first Flag Ceremony, Mr. Pines will move your trunks and duffels to your cabins."

"Except yours," Zach muttered before stepping away from Henry.

Ginny waited for the campers to settle

down. "Here's how our Olympics work. Dolphins and Seals try to get points for our activities and events, as well as for doing good things around camp."

"Like making our beds, right?" a girl around Benny's age asked. "My brother told me. And not screaming at the ferry horn. Only I did 'cause I forgot."

"And shooting a gazillion baskets in basketball," another boy added. "When my dad was a camper, his team won the Olympics. He was a good basketball player a long time ago."

"Up until this year, my groups won every single year," Kim announced. "I've been playing soccer and basketball since I was little. I won lots of points in the Camp Seagull Olympics. But not this year."

"How come?" one of the new campers wanted to know.

"I was a Junior Counselor for the Dolphins last session," Kim answered bitterly. "But we lost. Sports don't count as much anymore. The Olympics are *way* harder to win now."

"No fair," said the boy with the basketball player dad.

Ginny waited for the campers to quiet down. "Well, Rich and I did make a few changes in the Olympics. We wanted to make it easier for all campers to earn points, even those who aren't sports stars. So now campers think up new activities together that everyone can be good at — even if you don't play a sport."

"Like not talking too much, right?" Benny asked. "That's what my brother, Henry, told me. Only I talk a lot, so the Dolphins might not win for that."

Ginny tried not to laugh, but she couldn't help it. "Well, Benny, maybe you'll win the Make Somebody Laugh Award. Last session, the Seals thought up that activity."

Ginny held up a blue notebook. "In here, you'll find a list of fun Olympic activities from last session. You'll also get to add new ones when you go to your cabins later. Your counselor will make a list of all your ideas. Then each cabin will choose the one idea that best pulls the whole camp together and give it to me or Rich for our Big Idea Medal."

Rich continued where Ginny left off. "This medal is worth a hundred points to the winning side. Now we will officially begin camp with our first Camp Seagull Flag Ceremony."

The next thing the campers heard was a scratchy sound that filled the air. The campers covered their ears as the loud notes of a bugle blared out from a tape recorder.

"Hear ye! Hear ye, campers!" Rich called out over the loudspeaker. "Sorry we don't have a live bugler yet. We will when Henry Alden's bugle arrives with his trunk. What you just heard is the famous Camp Seagull bugle recording. Our new Junior Counselor Henry Alden will conduct the Flag Ceremony this session."

Henry stepped forward with the American flag and the Camp Seagull flag. As he had learned to do in the Scouts, Henry carefully unfolded the flags and fastened them to the ropes. As he guided the flags slowly up the pole, the campers watched in silence.

When both flags reached the top, Rich started the bugle tape again. The whole camp broke into a cheer.

"Let Camp Seagull begin!" Rich cried out over the cheers and the last notes of the crackling bugle tape.

The campers gave the Camp Seagull cheer. *"Crawk! Crawk!"* they all cried.

"Crawk! Crawk!" a seagull answered from its perch on the top of the flagpole.

After the Flag Ceremony, Ginny assigned each counselor to a group of campers.

"Let's find Violet," Henry suggested to Jessie and Benny. "I want to wish her luck before we go to our cabins."

They found Violet sitting cross-legged on the ground a few feet away from Kim Waters. Kim had a clipboard in front of her. She was speaking with her campers one by one.

When she saw her family, Violet scram-

bled to her feet. "My group is getting ready to go to our cabin," Violet said.

"I wish you were on the Dolphin team," Benny said. "Aldens like to stay together."

Violet's eyes darkened. "I know. At least you'll be with Henry. And I'll be near Jessie's cabin. Birch — that's the name of our cabin — is only two cabins away from hers. Maybe we can visit back and forth."

Jessie hugged Violet. "We'll all see one another at activities and meals, though not overnight."

"Violet Alden!" Kim yelled out. "Over here with the Seals. We have to get to Birch Cabin — on the double!"

Violet gave Jessie one last hug. " 'Bye. See you at dinner," she said.

Kim blew her whistle again. "The Seals sit together at meals," she told her campers. "Now what we're going to do is come up with the best Big Idea in the whole camp. This session, the Seals are going to win the Olympics. No matter what."

"Why is Kim so grouchy?" Benny asked. "I'm glad I'm a Dolphin."

"Maybe Kim wanted to be in the Dolphins again," Jessie guessed. "Well, time to go to our cabins with our campers. See you later, Benny. 'Bye, Henry."

CHAPTER 4

Boo!

Henry and Dave Baylor, a Senior Counselor, were in charge of the six- and seven-year-old Dolphin boys. They introduced themselves to the campers. Since Dave had work to do at the waterfront, Henry led the boys to the cabin on his own. "This way, Dolphins. Driftwood Cabin is just down the Interstate."

"Henry's kidding," Benny explained in case the other boys didn't get Henry's joke. "The Interstate doesn't go to Claw Island, just the Boo boat."

Henry noticed Zach pushing a cart piled high with duffel bags and trunks. "Hey, Zach, we're going the same way. That cart looks heavy. Want some help?"

"I don't need any help," Zach answered.

"Sorry about leaving our bags onshore," Henry said. "We didn't mean to make more work for you and your dad. When Dave comes back from the waterfront, maybe I can help you finish unloading the ferry."

"I told you, I don't need any help," Zach said. "I'm still in charge of luggage. You're in charge of the Flag Ceremony now. Let's keep it that way." Zach then pushed the cart so hard, it nearly tipped over on a tree root.

"How come Zach doesn't like you?" Benny whispered.

"I wish I knew," Henry said.

When Henry arrived at Driftwood Cabin with his group, Boo Pines was nailing some loose boards on the screen door.

"Boo!" one of the boys said.

Boo Pines didn't even look up.

"Let's not bother Mr. Pines," Henry told the boys. "First we'll unpack so we can make up our bunks."

"But you don't have a trunk," a boy named Sam said.

"Not yet," Henry said, "but it'll be here tomorrow. My bugle's in it. I'll teach you to play a few notes."

Benny was proud of his older brother. "Henry's the new bugle player and flag-raiser person," he announced.

"What about Zach?" Sam asked. "How come he's not doing it? That was his job last session."

Slam! Slam! All the boys, even Henry, jumped when the screen door banged so hard it shook the cabin.

"Something the matter?" Henry called out.

Out on the cabin porch, Boo shut the lid of his toolbox. The next sounds the boys heard were Boo's heavy work boots thumping down the steps. When Henry looked out, Boo had disappeared into the woods.

* * *

"Welcome to Cedar Cabin, Dolphins," Jessie began when her campers stepped inside. "It looks a little bare right now, but not for long. We'll fix it up so it's nice and cozy. My brothers and sister and I used to live in a boxcar in the woods. We made it like a real house."

"I wish our cabin was a boxcar," one of the campers said. "Will you tell us stories about living in the woods?"

"Lots of them," Jessie said, "including how our dog, Watch, found us. But first I need to get Lizzie Pines here. She's a day camper, but she's supposed to be in Cedar Cabin right now."

Jessie dug into her backpack. "Here's a piece of paper and a pencil, girls. I'll draw a squiggle on it. Then you girls pass it around and see if you can turn the squiggle into a picture by the time I get back with Lizzie. Here comes Sarah, our Senior Counselor. She'll stay with you while I fetch Lizzie. Hi, Sarah."

Outside, Jessie headed toward the ferry

landing. She spotted Lizzie and Zach talking.

"But I don't want to be a Dolphin," Jessie overheard Lizzie telling Zach when she got closer. "I want to be with Kim like last time. She said I could help her win the Olympics like we used to all the time before Ginny and Rich came. Maybe Kim will let me stay overnight in Birch Cabin. Then I can be an overnight camper like Dad promised."

Zach turned to his sister. "Look, Lizzie, you have to go along with the Aldens. Ginny and Rich are in charge now, not Dad. But there are lots of ways you can help Kim."

"Lizzie!" Jessie yelled out without coming closer. She didn't want Zach and Lizzie to know she had heard them talking about her. She motioned Lizzie to return to Cedar Cabin. Jessie walked back alone, wondering what was going on. What did Zach mean about Lizzie helping Kim?

"Squiggles was a good game for the girls," Sarah said when Jessie returned. "I have to run to the office. Be back soon."

A redheaded camper named Laura handed Jessie a sheet of paper. "Here's what we drew."

"A boxcar!" Jessie said, admiring the girls' drawing.

"Where's Lizzie?" Laura asked.

Jessie stuck her head out the door. Lizzie was coming toward the cabin. "She's right behind me. Let's carry in all of your trunks. I'll help you unpack now that Lizzie's on her way."

Lizzie was on her way — but not to Cedar Cabin. Instead, she stopped off at Birch Cabin.

All the Birch campers, except for Violet, had their trunks and duffels open. Violet was helping Kim unpack.

"Clean towels stay folded in the trunks," Kim told Violet. "I guess your sister and brother didn't read the rules. Especially the one saying not to leave your trunks on the beach."

Violet tried not to think about her neatly packed trunk sitting in Dark Harbor. She

looked up when Lizzie came in. "Did Jessie send you over to tell me something?"

"No," Lizzie answered. "I came to see Kim."

Kim turned around. "What's up, Lizzie? I was hoping you'd be in my group. I have to teach my campers everything, even not to forget their trunks."

"I have a message," Lizzie said. She handed Kim a piece of paper.

Kim read it over. "Hmmm. I guess it's okay. You'd better go to your own cabin now."

Lizzie didn't move. "Can't I stay a little longer? Or overnight? I'm sure my dad would let me. I could put a sleeping bag in the corner. I wouldn't take up much room."

Violet had an idea, but she was too shy to say anything right away. Finally she decided to speak up. "What if Lizzie and I switch? That way she could be a Seal and stay here in Birch since you're friends already."

Kim and Lizzie looked at each other.

"Please, Kim," Lizzie pleaded. "Can I stay here?"

Before Kim had time to answer, there was a knock on the cabin door.

"Come in," Kim called out. "Oh, hi, Sarah. I thought the Senior Counselors had a meeting in the office."

"It's over," Sarah said. She looked around until she spotted Lizzie sitting on Kim's bed. "Aha! I see you kidnapped one of my favorite campers," Sarah joked. "Lizzie, I think you forgot which cabin you were assigned to. You're with Jessie Alden and me over in Cedar. It's time to start the fun. We can't do that if one of the Dolphins in our pod is missing. Let's go, kiddo. Jessie's waiting."

Lizzie didn't move from Kim's bed. "But . . . but, we were just talking about Violet changing places and being a Dolphin instead. Then I could stay in Kim's group like last session."

"No way!" Sarah said, smiling. "Last session, you were such a great camper, I kept wishing you were on my team. And now you are. Off we go!"

Violet looked on as Sarah led Lizzie back to Cedar Cabin. She tried not to think about how strange everything seemed on her first night at camp. Jessie was just two cabins away, but that seemed as far away as Greenfield.

"I have an extra stuffed animal," one of the girls said, holding out a floppy fur rabbit. "You can borrow him until your trunk comes, Violet."

"If it comes," Kim said before shutting the lid of her own trunk.

CHAPTER 5

Footprints in the Sand

A spiral of blue-gray smoke arose from the campfire near Evergreen Lodge. The hamburger and hot dog smells from Camp Seagull's first cookout began to fade. Now that the day was nearly over, the first day of camp was fading, too.

Benny pulled his stick from the fire. On the end was a melted, golden brown marshmallow. He slid it between two graham crackers and a piece of chocolate. "Yum," he said after tasting his s'more treat. "Cookouts are my favorite."

"So are breakfast, lunch, and dinner," Henry kidded.

Jessie and Violet laughed at Henry's joke, along with the campers nearby.

"I'm glad Kim let us sit together for dessert," Violet told Jessie.

"Me, too," Jessie said. "Here, you can have my s'more. I'm full from our cookout," Jessie said. "Are you having fun with the Seals?"

Violet stared into the fire. "I'll like camp better when I can go on nature walks or start making pottery. Kim is upset with our cabin because of my trunk. She said I lost points for our team."

Jessie frowned. "Well, be sure to mention that since Henry and I are both Dolphins, our team will lose twice as many points for leaving our trunks behind. Ginny was a little upset, but she asked Mr. Pines to bring them to camp tomorrow morning when he drops off the day campers."

Violet wriggled her toes to warm them near the fire. "I'll still lose for cabin inspection. Kim's cross with me."

"That's just her way," Jessie said. "She's probably upset that Rich and Ginny changed the Olympics from sports to a lot of other activities. Don't worry. You'll help the Seals win with your crafts and the way you help other campers. Oh, listen," Jessie said, "it's the bugle tape again."

"I have a few announcements before Henry takes down the flags for the night," Rich began. "Counselors, remember to walk your campers to the dock at seven-twenty. Mr. Pines will have the ferry ready to bring the day campers back to Dark Harbor for the night."

Benny was glad to hear this. "I like camp," he said to Jessie, "but I like seeing Grandfather 's'more.' "

"Good one," Jessie said, laughing at Benny's joke. "Uh-oh. S'more bugle music is coming on. Let's stand up for Flag Ceremony."

Henry walked over to the flagpole and lowered the camp flags as the campers watched quietly. When the flags reached the bottom of the ropes, everyone cheered for

Henry. He carefully folded the flags for the next day and brought them to Evergreen Lodge.

Jessie's and Henry's Dolphins gathered near one another to walk back to their cabins. The sun slid behind the mountains. The wind picked up and whistled through the pine trees.

"Have you seen Lizzie?" Jessie asked Sarah, the Senior Counselor. "She keeps disappearing on me."

"I saw her with Kim walking to the Bogs — you know, the camp bathrooms," Sarah said. "Go ahead with the other girls. I'll make sure Lizzie gets to the cabin."

"Brrr. I'm an ice cube," Benny said as all the Dolphins made their way through the woods.

"How are we going to stay warm in the cabins when it's so dark and cold?" a girl named Daisy asked Jessie.

"At lights-out, we'll close the shutters and the doors and get under the covers," Jessie said. "The cabins are small. Our body heat will warm them right up."

"Not my body heat," Benny said. "I'm going to be at Grandfather's hotel in a big old bed with lots of quilts."

"Sssh," Henry said. He didn't want his overnight campers to start thinking about the warm beds they left behind at home. "Our cabin will be snug and warm."

"And dark," one little boy said as the groups walked deeper into the woods. "The lights from Evergreen Lodge are getting far away."

"But the light from my flashlight is right here," Henry told his group. He turned on the big flashlight Mrs. McGregor had given him to keep in his backpack. "See?"

The flashlight helped the children find their way through the woods. Unfortunately, the light made the children see shadows everywhere, too.

Daisy stayed close to Jessie. "I wish you'd brought your dog, Watch," she said as everyone huddled near one another on the walk to the cabins. "Look. Now Seal Rock looks like Monster Rock again."

Jessie and Henry looked out over the water. They didn't say anything right away. Indeed, now that evening was coming on, the dark, smooth rock did look like the back of some giant creature in the water.

"It's only the mist and the ocean moving," Jessie said in her soothing voice, "not Monster — I mean, Seal Rock."

The Dolphins weren't far from their cabins when they heard a branch crack in the woods.

"Ooooh! What was that?" Benny said. "Did a tree fall down?"

Jessie stepped ahead. "Watch my campers, Henry. I'll run ahead."

Jessie found her own flashlight. She walked quickly for about ten feet. She noticed a broken tree branch close to Cedar Cabin. She dragged it off the path and walked back to her campers. Jessie shined her flashlight on the damp sandy path. Daisy, still nervous, was right by her side.

"Look!" Daisy screamed.

The other campers screamed, too. They grabbed on to Jessie's arms and legs.

"There, there, girls. Why are you screaming?" she asked her jittery campers.

Daisy pointed to the ground in front of them. "Footprints! Monster footprints!"

Jessie looked closely at the ground. She wanted to believe Daisy's eyes were playing tricks. Then she saw what Daisy saw — huge claw prints, nearly a foot wide, one in front of the other.

Jessie's mind raced. She needed to stay calm for her Dolphins. She waved her flashlight around the nearby woods. She saw two pairs of eyes flash back. But they weren't monster eyes, unless the monsters were wearing Camp Seagull T-shirts. The figures ran off into the woods.

"Somebody played a silly trick on us so we'd scream," Jessie said. "Sarah says one team does that at the end of the week to make the other team lose points. But it's not supposed to happen the first few nights. Our monster didn't come from the ocean but from Camp Seagull.

"And we won't scream again," she went on. "We just have to find the monsters who played the trick."

When the girls arrived at their cabin, Sarah was waiting. "I didn't find Lizzie. I thought she caught up with you. So it *was* you guys screaming outside. That's what Kim said, anyway. She just raced in here to remind me to take away points for screaming."

"Was she wearing a camp T-shirt?" Jessie asked.

"We're all wearing camp T-shirts," Sarah answered with a laugh.

"I wish we weren't going to lose points for screaming," Jessie said. Then she cheered up. "I just thought of something."

A couple of girls pulled on Jessie's sleeves. "What? What?" they asked.

"If we find the person who made the monster footprints, that person's team will lose points for scaring people," Jessie said. "Not that we're scared — right, Dolphins?"

"Right!" the Dolphin girls cheered.

CHAPTER 6

Trouble for Jessie

Jessie's cabin soon sounded as if it were filled with chipmunks. The Cedar Cabin campers were settling in.

"There you are," Jessie said when Lizzie finally showed up for the cabin meeting. "We had a bit of excitement in the woods. Somebody tried to scare us, but we didn't get scared — not too much, anyway. Right, girls?" Jessie asked. "Come on in, Lizzie," Jessie continued. "Leave your sneakers outside, though. They're all wet and sandy.

And next time, stay with our cabin group, okay?"

Lizzie stepped on the porch to remove her sneakers. When she came back, she stood in the doorway barefoot. The other girls arranged themselves on the beds and the floor close to Jessie. Lizzie stayed where she was.

"Okay, Dolphins, let's talk about some ideas you might have for the Big Idea Medal," Jessie began. "I'll write down your ideas. After that, we'll vote on one to give Ginny and Rich."

"I know," Daisy began. "We could have Be Nice Days. We would put slips of paper with our names on them in a box and choose one every day. Then we all would do nice things for that person on her day."

"Or at lights-out time, I could sing my favorite song," another girl piped up. "That's to help anyone who can't fall asleep. My mom does that. Is that good, Jessie?"

"It sure is. I'll write it down on my list."

Jessie found a notepad and began writing the girls' suggestions.

"Can we write down sharing chocolate?" a girl in pigtails asked.

The girls giggled, even Jessie.

Lizzie Pines didn't giggle, though. "Food is not allowed in the cabins," she told everyone. "Junior Counselors have to know the rules."

"Lizzie's right," Jessie said. "No chocolate or any food in Cedar Cabin. Thank you, Lizzie."

"Where's your trunk?" Daisy asked when she noticed Jessie only had a backpack on her bed. "Didn't you bring one?"

Jessie felt her whole face get red, even her ears.

Before Jessie could explain what happened, Lizzie interrupted. "The Aldens left their stuff at the ferry. Cedar Cabin is going to lose points."

"What about your pj's and teddy bear?" Daisy asked Jessie. She double-checked that her own pajamas and teddy bear were right there.

"I'm really sorry I let you girls down by forgetting my trunk," Jessie said. "But maybe I can help make up for it. While I was listing your ideas, I thought of a way to combine all of your suggestions into one super Big Idea."

"How?" some of the girls asked at the same time.

"Me and My Buddy could be the name for all of your ideas," Jessie said. "One camper who's good or strong at something helps another camper who isn't. Since everybody's good at something, and everybody needs a little help at other things, we all get to help our Buddies or have a Buddy help us."

After the Dolphins added more ideas, Jessie tapped her pencil against the wooden beam over her bed. "Hear! Hear!" Jessie began. She read off the list: " 'Teach Someone to Make Her Bed. Teach Somebody How to Do Something Hard. Help a Friend to Not Be Afraid of the Dark.' "

Jessie kept writing until her girls couldn't think of anything else. "Those will all be part of our Me and My Buddy Big Idea."

The chattering started up again as the girls talked about who could be Buddies for each other. They didn't notice that not everyone was still in the cabin. A few minutes later, they heard a knock on the door.

Ginny stepped into Cedar Cabin. "Inspection." She began to look around. She noticed how tidy everything was. All the trunks were shut. All the beds were made. All the sand and cobwebs had been swept away.

"Nice work, Dolphins," Ginny said. "Except for Jessie's wayward trunk, I'm giving you full points for a perfect cabin. Then Ginny noticed everything wasn't quite perfect in Cedar Cabin. "Goodness, Jessie, where's Lizzie?"

All eyes turned to Jessie. She got up from her bed and ran to the porch. "She was here just a second ago." Jessie looked down. Lizzie's sneakers were gone, with Lizzie in them!

"I'll need to talk with you about this,"

Ginny said. "I'm in a bit of a rush, but I'll wait here a few minutes while you go find her. Check the Bogs first."

Jessie headed to the girls' bathrooms. When she arrived, several of Kim's Seals were busy filling a water bucket with soapy water. Violet spotted Jessie in the mirror.

"Kim told us we have to wash down the cabin floor," Violet explained. "She said we didn't have any good activities for the Big Idea. I guess she wants us to get lots of points for making our cabin super clean. We have to hurry."

"Sorry," Jessie said. "Did you happen to see Lizzie in here?"

Violet nodded. "Not here, but she was in Birch when we all came to the Bogs. Want me to get her?"

"No, I'll go," Jessie answered.

Jessie stopped by Birch Cabin. Kim looked up. "If you're looking for Lizzie, she left for the ferry."

Jessie got to the point. "We need to talk with Lizzie about not coming here without

telling me. If we both talk to her, we can explain that the groups have to stay together for safety reasons."

"Fine," Kim said. "But I can't help it if she wants to be in my group and not yours. Anyway, she went to see her brother and her dad. It's not a big deal."

But it did turn out to be a big deal. When Jessie came back to Cedar Cabin alone, Ginny stepped onto the porch. "Jes-sie, it's time for the day campers to go back to Dark Harbor. Camp Seagull isn't just about the Olympics. It's also about responsibility. Lizzie is your responsibility."

Jessie looked down at her flip-flops. First her trunk was missing. Now one of her campers was missing. "I know. She already went to the ferry. I . . . uh . . . guess we'll meet her there."

Ginny's face grew very serious. "After the ferry leaves, ask Sarah to watch the cabin. Then please take some time to go over the rules about knowing where your campers are at all times. It's our most important safety rule."

To Jessie, every word that Ginny said felt like a stone falling on her head. "I know. I'm so sorry. I'll be much more careful."

Jessie walked slightly ahead of her Dolphins as they made their way to the ferry. She didn't want them to see that she was upset.

Henry's group caught up with Jessie's.

"What's the matter, Jessie?" Henry asked.

Jessie took a deep breath to steady her voice. "Lizzie left the cabin without telling me. I overheard her tell Zach she wants to be in Kim's cabin. Then I didn't know where she was when Ginny came by. When she and Kim don't follow the rules, I'm the one who looks like I don't know what I'm doing, and my campers lose points, too."

Henry nodded. "Same here, Jessie. Only Zach's the one who makes me feel like I shouldn't be here — like he's in charge of Camp Seagull or something. He won't do anything with the Dolphins."

CHAPTER 7

The Disappearing Flags

The next day, Henry Alden didn't need an alarm clock to wake up. When Dave Baylor, the Senior Counselor, arrived to supervise the campers in Driftwood Cabin, Henry was already up and dressed.

"Rich was right about you Aldens being early birds," Dave said. "I'll make sure you get points toward the Rise and Shine Medal."

Henry grinned. "We could use those points. I left my trunk at the ferry in Dark

Harbor," he told Dave. "I slept in my clothes, so that saved time. I always get up early, though."

Dave sat down on Henry's cot. "So does everybody around here. Just blast Rich's tape recorder with that bugle music. I guarantee campers will jump out of their beds like bedbugs. I'll get everybody in Driftwood Cabin around the flagpole by seven. That's when Boo brings over the day campers on the ferry. See you."

Camp Seagull was still quiet when Henry walked toward Evergreen Lodge. On the way, he went by Cedar Cabin, hoping to see Jessie. Like her brother, she was an early bird.

Sure enough, she was up and saw Henry go by. She stuck her head out the window over her bed.

"Hi, Jess," Henry whispered. "I see you slept in your clothes, too. I sure didn't like having my campers find out I left my trunk in Dark Harbor. Makes me look as if I don't know what I'm doing."

"I know," Jessie said miserably. "I can't

stop thinking about last night when Ginny told me to look over the rules about watching the campers. I already know the rules. The problem is, I can't get Lizzie and Kim to follow them. I'll see you later."

Henry went to the storage room when he got to Evergreen Lodge. He found the tape recorder and an extension cord. He plugged it in and brought the recorder outside. He pressed the start button. Then he blocked both ears.

The awful recorded bugle music drowned out the peaceful sounds of the ocean lapping in the distance. Two seagulls on the roof of Evergreen Lodge flew away in a hurry.

Henry checked his watch, then he returned to the storage room. "Where are those flags, anyway?" Henry said to himself as he looked around. "I know I put them in here last night after the campfire." He checked the shelves, then the closet. Nothing.

By this time, Ginny and Rich had arrived at their office.

"Morning, Henry," Rich said. "Mr. Pines will be here with your trunks when the ferry arrives. After the Flag Ceremony, you can bring them to the cabins."

Henry still felt bad about the missing trunks. He sure didn't want to tell the Gullens that the flags were missing, too.

"It'll be great to hear you blow a real bugle when your trunk gets here," Ginny told Henry. "That tape is pretty worn out by now. Our cat hides under the bed when she hears it."

"So do some of our campers!" Rich said with a laugh. "Live or recorded, the bugle wake-up is a Camp Seagull tradition."

Ginny smiled at Henry. "You did a nice job during the Flag Ceremony after the campfire last night, Henry. This morning the campers will watch the flag-raising, then sing the Camp Seagull song." Ginny paused. "What's the matter, Henry? Are you nervous? Don't be. You'll do fine again."

Henry shifted from one foot to the other. "Well, you see . . . actually, I can't find the flags right now. I remember folding them after the ceremony last night. I thought I put them away with the tape recorder. But now they're not in the storage room."

Henry noticed a tiny frown pass over Ginny's face. This was the same look she'd given the Aldens when she discovered their trunks had been left behind.

"Oh, dear," Ginny said quietly. "Rich and I will look around here. Run back to your cabin. See if you brought them there by mistake."

As campers streamed toward the flagpole, Henry dashed off to his cabin. Those flags just had to be there!

"Where're you going?" Henry's Driftwood Dolphins wanted to know when they saw him going the other way.

Jessie and Violet wanted to know the same thing when Henry passed by.

"Henry, it's almost seven o'clock," Jessie said. "Did you forget something in your cabin?"

Henry pulled Jessie to the side. "Did you notice what I did with the flags last night? I can't find them anywhere. I'm almost a hundred percent sure I put them in Evergreen Lodge with the tape recorder. But they're not there now."

Jessie was upset for her brother. "I feel terrible. There was so much going on that I didn't see where you went or what you did. Sorry."

Zach came over to Jessie and Henry. "Your trunks are by the dock. Aren't you supposed to be in charge of the Flag Ceremony right now?" He checked his watch. "It's in ten minutes. Flag Ceremony is always at seven o'clock in the morning — unless Ginny and Rich changed that, too."

Jessie's Dolphins looked confused by the delay. "Come along," she said, leading her campers toward the flagpole.

"Hurry up!" Kim ordered her group. "You can't be late for Flag Ceremony or we'll lose points."

Henry tried not to panic. Still, his heart was racing. "I have only a few minutes." He burst into Driftwood Cabin. He checked around as best he could in the short time he had. "It's no use. I know I didn't bring those flags here."

He felt sick inside. He didn't want to let down the whole camp. All he wanted was to set his eyes on those two flags. He wanted to listen to the hush that would come over the campers as he raised the flags to begin the day.

He turned back toward Evergreen Lodge. His legs felt like wooden blocks. As he ran back, he had a new dark thought: *The Dolphins are probably going to have a trillion points taken away from them because I lost those flags.*

When he came to the clearing, Henry saw the expectant campers waiting for him. The ferry had brought in the day campers. He saw Benny waving.

Henry's mind slowed down. What was he going to say to everyone? How could he tell them that, for the first time ever, Camp Seagull wouldn't be starting the day with the Flag Ceremony?

As he was trying to come up with the words, Jessie appeared. Trailing behind were some of the Cedar Cabin Dolphins. Jessie was grinning from ear to ear.

"Did you find the flags?" Henry asked, barely able to get the words out.

Daisy handed Henry two stiff posters. "Here. Jessie told us what to do. She found some poster board in the arts and crafts room, and markers, too. We drew the flags on them. The flags aren't very pretty. We only had time to draw a bunch of lines."

Henry couldn't believe his eyes when he saw the two hand-drawn flags. One of them had a bird in the middle that almost looked like the one on the Camp Seagull flag. The other had stars and stripes — most of them, anyway.

"Thanks," Henry said to the Cedar Cabin Dolphins. "These are the nicest flags I've ever seen."

Rich made a move to start up the bugle tape. "They're almost as nice as the real ones, Henry," he said, "wherever they are. Ginny just gave the Dolphins twenty-five points for the Quick Thinking Award. Of course, losing the flags cost you twenty

points, but you Dolphins made a five-point gain anyway." With that, Rich blasted the recorded bugle music to get everyone's attention. It was time for the famous Camp Seagull Flag Ceremony.

Henry attached the handmade flags to the ropes and pulled them gently. Up went the Stars and Stripes. Up went the Camp Seagull flag, which was soon flapping in the wind.

"Crawk! Crawk!" some of the campers cried when the flag reached the top.

Everyone cheered the Cedar Cabin Dolphins, who had saved the day. Then they gave a cheer for Henry Alden, to make him feel better.

Well, not quite everyone. When Jessie looked around to check on Lizzie, she noticed she was over with Zach and Kim near the dock. They were sitting on the Aldens' trunks, and they weren't cheering at all.

CHAPTER 8

The Switch

After the Flag Ceremony, Henry and Jessie fetched their trunks. They quickly dropped them off at their cabins. In no time, they caught up to everyone heading to Evergreen Lodge for breakfast. It was Blueberry Pancake Day. Nobody wanted to miss that!

Jessie's and Henry's tables were next to each other. Luckily for Violet, Kim's table was nearby as well. The Aldens liked meeting new campers. But they also liked seeing one another at camp.

Jessie turned around to see how Benny was doing. "Are you going to eat that whole stack of blueberry pancakes?" she asked.

Benny wiped some sticky maple syrup from the corners of his mouth. "Grandfather said I should only have a tiny piece of toast in case my stomach did flip-flops on the ferry. I saved being hungry for breakfast at camp."

"I guess you did, by the look of your plate," Henry said. "Now the Dolphins don't have to worry about losing points for the No Food on the Floor Award."

A loud drumming sound boomed over the noisy dining hall. Ginny was onstage banging a metal serving spoon against a metal soup pot from the camp kitchen.

"I think Ginny and Rich are about to announce who won the Big Idea," Jessie said. "I hope the Dolphins have a good chance."

Daisy squeezed Jessie's hand. "I can't wait. Maybe our cabin will win. Do you want to know what our idea is?" Daisy asked a boy Dolphin at Henry's table.

"Shhhh, no telling," Jessie told Daisy just in time.

After everyone finally quieted down, Ginny tapped the microphone. "I know you're all eager to find out who the Big Idea winner is. We won't keep you waiting any longer. As your counselors told you, for our new Olympics we asked all the cabins to think up ways to make Camp Seagull the best ever. The Big Idea Medal is for the best of the bunch — the idea that pulls the whole camp together."

Ginny stepped away from the microphone so Rich could speak. "We were up half the night trying to decide on the winner. There were so many great entries, we'd have to run Camp Seagull all year 'round to try them all out. Now, after I announce the idea we chose, I'd like the winning counselor to come up. Drumroll, please."

Ginny banged on the soup pot again. The campers banged on their tables with their silverware. Evergreen Lodge was jumping!

"And the winner is . . . Me and My Buddy!" Rich yelled into the microphone.

"We won! We won!" the Dolphins at Jessie's table yelled.

"We won! We won!" the Seals at Kim's table yelled.

Ginny banged the soup pot again to get everyone's attention. "For the first time this summer, we have two identical outstanding ideas," Ginny announced when everyone quieted down. "Because Me and My Buddy is so special, I'd like to recognize Jessie's Dolphins. Come up here and take a bow, Jessie."

Jessie stepped onstage, confused. The audience was confused, too. Only a few campers clapped.

"Now let's hear it for the Seals, who submitted their idea first," Ginny cried. "Come on up for your group, Kim."

"What? No fair," one Dolphin after another muttered.

Jessie tried to say something to make her campers feel better, but her lips wouldn't move.

Ginny tapped the microphone with her pencil. "Now, now. Let's all be good sports. It's only fair to give the medal to the group that came up with the idea first."

Rich took the microphone. "I hereby award one hundred points to the Seals, along with a special banner to the girls of Birch Cabin." Rich shook Kim's hand, then gave her the Cabin of the Week banner. "The Seals move to the front in the Olympics. Let's hear it for the Seals and for Birch!"

The Birch Cabin Seals ran to the stage. They helped Kim hold up the banner.

"Go, Seals!" the Seals roared.

When the cheering died down, Rich explained the winning idea and then made the morning announcements. "Now it's time to clean your tables and bring your plates to the kitchen. Then you'll return to your cabins for morning cabin inspection. After that, everyone goes to activities. Meanwhile, we hope you will find Buddies and Buddies will find you to help each other the rest of the week."

The Dolphins were quiet as they cleared their tables.

Jessie wiped up every drip and speck. She didn't want the Dolphins to fall further behind. "I'm so sorry I somehow let you down," Jessie said to the girls as they were cleaning up. "I never thought someone else would come up with our same idea and that I should have gotten it to Ginny before the Seals did."

Jessie's Dolphins were too disappointed to say anything.

"Dolphins," Henry said to make everyone feel better, "the Seals are ahead now, but this is only the beginning of camp."

"I'll be your Buddy, Jessie," Daisy said as the group walked back to the cabins for inspection.

This made Jessie smile. "If there's a Big Heart Award, you'll win it, Daisy." She turned to the other Dolphins. "Here are your schedules for today's activities. Start walking to the first activity. Henry and I will meet you there in a few minutes."

"Can I stay with you?" Benny asked his brother and sister. "Henry gave me my schedule already. Look, here comes Violet."

The four Aldens stood on the porch without speaking. They looked at the campers below, who were excited to start the day. Were they ever going to feel that way about Camp Seagull?

"We just arrived at camp," Jessie began, "and too many things keep happening that don't make sense. First our trunks are left behind. Next you can't find the flags, Henry. Then Kim's group somehow comes up with the same idea as the Dolphins."

"And Lizzie doesn't obey and keeps on disappearing," Henry said. "Don't forget that."

"Right," Jessie went on. "I have a feeling she and Kim tried to scare the Dolphins with the monster footprints so we'd lose points for screaming. But the big thing is what just happened. I have a feeling Kim somehow got Me and My Buddy from our group. But how?"

Henry looked at Violet. "I know you can't really talk about how your cabin decided on its Big Idea. But did anything happen that seemed suspicious?"

Jessie stopped her sister before she could

answer. "Violet, you really shouldn't say anything about this."

Violet wanted to help, but she stopped herself. She knew Jessie was right.

Henry shook his head and said, "There's got to be a way to find out if Kim copied you."

Jessie turned to Violet. "It's time to send you on your way," she said. "It wouldn't be fair for you to hear our plans for solving this mystery."

Violet walked slowly back to her cabin.

Benny looked over at Henry. Henry's eyebrows were scrunched together. Benny knew what that meant. Henry was cooking up a plan.

Henry began, "On Costume Night, we'll let the Dolphins think we're going to dress up one way, but we'll really have secret costumes!"

"You mean, we'll tell everybody we're going to be ghosts, but then we'll be pirates?" Benny asked.

"Exactly!" Henry said. "The only problem is figuring out how to let Ginny and Rich know what our real costumes are ahead of time."

"We could give them a letter in an envelope beforehand," Jessie suggested, "and tell them not to open it until after the costume contest. If somebody shows up with the same costumes, then they'll know who the copycats are."

"Not the Aldens," Benny said. "We're not copycats."

"Let's do it," Henry said.

CHAPTER 9

Secret Disguises

For the next two days, Henry, Jessie, and Benny were busy every minute. They worked hard to win points and to pull close to the Seals in the Olympics.

The Dolphins won the most points for all the cabin inspections. They picked up the First One in the Freezing Water at Swimming Lessons Medal. When they decorated their fruits like circus clowns, they won the Dress Up Your Favorite Fruit Medal. Benny picked up ten points all by himself. He made people laugh more than any other camper. His table didn't lose a single point for dropping food on the floor, either. As the week went on, the Dolphins were catching up to the Seals.

Jessie checked the points board one morning after the Flag Ceremony. "I sure wish you could find those flags, Henry. Maybe Rich and Ginny would give the Dolphins back some of the points you lost after they disappeared."

Henry groaned. "Uh, don't mention those. My cabin is trying to sew another seagull flag, but they haven't gotten very far. They're too busy working on their costumes. Plus I'm busy working on two sets of costumes for the Dolphin boys — the secret ones and the fake ones."

"Well, I'd help you, but I'm busy with our girls' costumes," Jessie whispered. "I stayed up half the night with my flashlight by my side making a lobster head out of a cardboard box. I found some old oven mitts the kitchen was throwing out. So I made claws out of them. I can only work on the costumes while my campers are asleep. I'm so tired I can hardly keep my eyes open."

"Well, I've got a little free time now," Henry told Jessie. "Dave's at the playing field with our campers. That means I'll have the cabin to myself to finish the secret costumes. I'm making underwater creature headpieces out of boxes I've been sneaking from the office trash."

"My costume's easy," Benny whispered so no one walking by would overhear. "The other kids think I'm making an astronaut suit from the gray sweatshirt Dave gave me. But it's going to be a whale outfit."

"Sounds good," Henry told Benny. "My campers are going wild on their space outfits. Wait until I tell them they have to be lobsters and sharks and clams, not space aliens. I hid the masks and headpieces way under the cabin. Rich and Ginny never check there during cabin inspection. We still haven't had a surprise inspection yet, so we have to be on the lookout all the time."

"What about the letter to Ginny and Rich?" Jessie asked.

"Done!" Henry pulled a sheet of lined

paper from his pocket. He looked around. "Good. Nobody's coming. I'll read it to you."

Dear Ginny and Rich,

The Dolphins would like to register our idea for Costume Night ahead of time. Everybody thinks we're going to be space creatures. But we will really show up as underwater creatures.

Yours truly,
Henry Alden

"That sounds fine," Jessie said. "Here's the envelope I wrote. It says: 'To Be Opened After Costume Night Begins.' We'll give it to Ginny and Rich tomorrow."

"I wish we could tell Violet about our plan," Benny said when he saw her walking toward him. "I like it when we all have the same secret."

Violet seemed shy around her sister and brothers now that they had secrets from her. "Hi," she said. "Is it okay to visit with you?"

Henry gave his sister a hug. "Sure thing,

Violet. Being on different teams isn't much fun."

Benny had a question. "What are your costumes?"

Violet grinned, then shook her head. "Teams aren't allowed to tell each other their ideas."

"Can you tell if Kim picked one of your ideas?" Benny asked. "You always made the best costumes for the Greenfield Halloween parade."

Violet nodded. "I did give Kim one idea. We started on it. But since your team has gotten so many points in the last couple of days, she was afraid my idea wasn't strong enough to win. All of a sudden, she came up with something else. That's what our cabin is working on now. I can't say what it is."

Henry was proud of his sister for keeping her cabin's secret. "Okay, Violet. Hey, there's Zach. We'd better all leave.

"Oh, hi," Henry said when Zach came out of the camp office with an armload of papers. "Anything for me?"

As usual, Zach answered Henry with as few words as possible. "No."

Henry turned to Benny. "Let's go to the playing field. I told Dave I'd drop you off. Afterward I'll be at the cabin."

"Can't I help finish some of those shark heads?" Benny asked.

"Shhh." Henry pointed to Zach. He was still nearby, reading notices on the camp bulletin board.

"Oops," Benny whispered before he and Henry left.

After dropping off Benny at the field, Henry returned to Driftwood Cabin. He looked around, and then he crawled under the cabin. He had hidden several trash bags filled with cardboard, paint, and materials from the arts and crafts room. He was still under the cabin with his legs sticking out when he heard Rich's voice nearby.

"Surprise inspection!" Rich announced, laughing. "I know you Dolphins want to win the Olympics, but you don't have to clean under the cabin, whoever you are."

"Ouch!" Henry cried as he bumped his

head crawling out backward. "It's me."

Rich gave Henry a once-over. "Henry, good thing this is cabin inspection, not Junior Counselor inspection. You're covered with dirt and pine needles."

Henry looked down at himself. His knees and elbows were sandy. He had cobwebs in his hair. There were pine needles stuck to his clothes. "Sorry, Rich."

"I didn't expect to find anyone here," Rich said. "Everybody's at activities. What were you doing under the cabin, anyway? Did you drop something down there?"

"Oh, I . . . uh . . . had a free period," Henry began, "and came here to work on our costumes. I, uh . . . lost a sewing needle through the floorboards."

Rich thought this was funny. "Did you really expect to find something that small down there, Henry? Ginny and I should check under all the cabins. That's probably where all our lost things go."

This made Henry nervous. "Uh, no. There's nothing but pine needles under there." He brushed himself off and went up the porch stairs. He hoped Rich didn't get any more ideas about checking under the cabin. "I'll stand out on the porch while you do the surprise inspection. I don't want to mess up the cabin after we just cleaned it."

Rich went inside. "Looking good, Henry. Beds tight. Trunks under the bed. Towels hung up on the railing. Flags on the . . . bed! The flags! What are they doing on your bed?"

Henry forgot about messing up the cabin. He raced inside. What was Rich talking about? "My campers were trying to make a new Camp Seagull flag, but they didn't get very far."

Rich unfolded the large cloth flag he'd found on Henry's bed. "I'd say your campers did a pretty good likeness of the camp seagull. Take a look."

Henry couldn't believe his eyes. "That's the real flag that was missing!"

"Here's the other one," Rich said, unrolling the Stars and Stripes. "How come you were keeping them in your cabin? These belong in Evergreen Lodge."

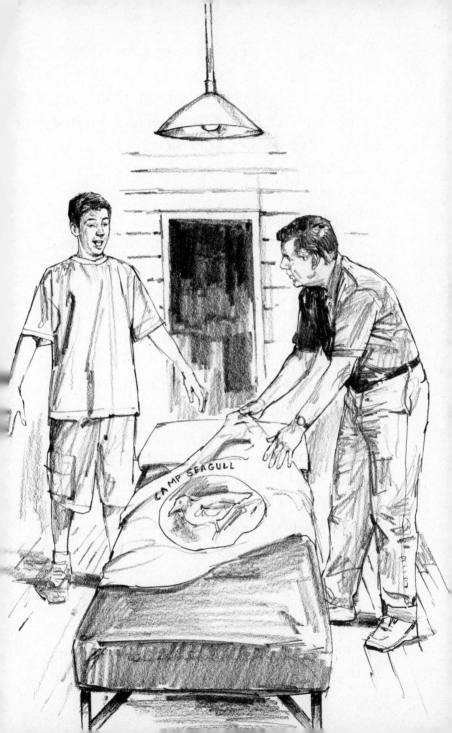

Henry shook his head in confusion. "They weren't here this morning. Honest, Rich. I have no idea how they landed on my bed. I've been searching for them ever since they disappeared."

Rich was smiling.

"What?" Henry asked, more confused than ever.

"Well, now that the flags turned up on your bed, I'm going to give you back ten of the twenty points you lost for losing them," Rich told Henry.

Henry gave Rich a thumbs-up. "Whew! That's a relief. Thanks."

"But," Rich went on, still grinning, "you lose ten points for having stuff on your bed — the flags — and a pile of pine needles and a trail of sand on the floor. Now you can go back to crawling around under the cabin. Funny way to spend your free period."

After Rich left with the flags and his Olympics clipboard, Henry sat down on his bed. That's when he noticed something in the cabin mailbox on the wall. A piece of paper was sticking out that hadn't been there in the morning.

Henry took the paper. "A schedule change," he said. Then an idea hit him. "I bet Zach delivered this when I went to the playing field with Benny," Henry said to himself. "I wonder if he had anything to do with those flags showing up."

CHAPTER 10

Costume Night

The girls in Birch Cabin gathered around Violet. "Can you be my costume Buddy?" a girl named Maggie asked. "You helped me with the candy dish I made in pottery. I need a Buddy again for my costume. Kim's too busy."

Kim raced around the cabin looking for pins and glue and scissors for her own costume. "Hurry up with the girls, Violet," she said. "We have to be at Evergreen Lodge soon. I want to be at the front of the costume parade. The Styrofoam on my headpiece doesn't look right. I'm supposed to be a scary alien, but I look like a television set."

Kim wasn't the friendliest counselor at Camp Seagull. The girls weren't sure whether or not to laugh. Finally, they couldn't help it. Kim *did* look like a Styrofoam television set, not a space alien.

Kim finally looked pleased with her campers. "Well, now I know I'm going to win for best costume idea. Usually campers just dress up like ghosts or witches, but being space aliens is much better. Uh-oh! Where's the spaceship? You need to put on your spaceship, Violet. Oh, I'm ready to scream, but I can't, or we'll lose points."

Violet calmly walked to the broom closet. "Here it is."

"It's beautiful, Violet," Maggie said.

Indeed, the spaceship Violet had made was a silvery beauty. She had covered two long sheets of poster board with silver paint. There was an opening for her face and a spaceship window drawn around it. All Violet had to do was sandwich herself between the two sides.

"It's nice," Kim said. This was the first time she'd said anything kind to Violet.

In Driftwood Cabin, Henry had his hands full with some very confused Dolphins.

"Why am I a lobster?" one boy asked as Henry put on red gloves that were supposed to be claws. "I thought I was going to be a space alien."

Benny's eyes grew larger than usual. "Somebody might copy our idea. That's why we made something different — to fool them."

"Who?" the lobster camper asked.

"We don't know for sure," Henry said. "So we decided to change into secret costumes. Now promise you won't bite anyone."

The sea creatures laughed. They had fun waving their cardboard fins and claws at one another.

Cedar Cabin was filling up with underwater creatures, including a goldfish, a horseshoe crab, and even a scary stingray.

"We just have to wait for Lizzie to get here," Jessie said. "She's helping her dad with the ferry. He's making a few trips to bring out all the parents and grandparents for Costume Night."

"Lizzie's going to be surprised when she finds out she's a sea turtle, not an astronaut," Daisy said.

Jessie smiled as she put on her own dolphin headpiece. "Shhh, I think she's coming up the steps."

"What's going on?" Lizzie asked when she stepped inside. "Am I in the wrong cabin or something?"

Jessie found the poster-board turtle shell she had made in secret. "It's a sea turtle costume. See, you just tie it around your waist."

"We're supposed to be aliens, not sea turtles!" Lizzie cried. "I promised."

"Promised whom?" Jessie asked in a serious voice.

Before Lizzie could answer, the girls heard more footsteps.

"Shut the door," Jessie said. "It might be one of the Seals coming to take a look. "Who is it?" she asked when there was a knock at the door.

"Benny the Whale and Henry the Shark," a boy's voice answered. "Open up, or we'll swallow your cabin!"

The girls burst into giggles.

Jessie opened the door.

"Time to go," Henry said, speaking through his shark head. "The rest of my cabin is outside."

"Hey, where's your costume, Lizzie?" Benny asked. "Aren't you going to be a sea turtle like Jessie told me?"

The sea turtle costume lay on Lizzie's bed, untouched. Instead, she grabbed her astronaut helmet. "I'm not going to Costume Night as a sea turtle. This is my costume."

The campers entered Evergreen Lodge cabin group by cabin group. Kim led her Seals at the front of the costume parade. She had a big confident smile when the audience cheered the space aliens. The Birch Cabin campers stepped to the side to watch the rest of the parade.

Pirates and goblins and even a couple of campers dressed as Monster Rock paraded in. Campers cheered for one another.

When Henry's and Jessie's Dolphins came in, the cheers were the loudest of all.

Then Benny tapped Jessie's dolphin fin to get her attention. "Look at Kim. Her face is all red. She's not clapping anymore. She's too mad to clap."

"What's going on, Lizzie?" Kim asked when the Dolphins passed the Seals. "You told me the kids in your cabin were coming as space aliens!"

The Dolphins turned around. Lizzie had joined the parade, after all — not as an astronaut but as a sea turtle! She actually liked the sea turtle costume better.

Ginny and Rich had been standing near Kim's group and had overheard her question to Lizzie.

"What do you mean, Kim?" Ginny asked. "Did Lizzie tell you what the Dolphins

were planning to wear? Please explain your-
self."

Kim's space alien headpiece fell sideways
on her head. She sputtered and tried to
straighten it out.

"Does anyone know what's going on?"
Ginny asked. "I'm going to have Rich make
an announcement to the audience that we
are serving refreshments first. In the mean-
time, I want to get to the bottom of this."

Jessie stepped away from her campers.
"Did you find the letter we put in your
mailbox, Ginny? It might explain this mix-
up better than what anyone tells you."

Rich overheard this. He handed Ginny
the Aldens' letter. Ginny read it over and
looked at Henry and Jessie, puzzled. "You
mean you *knew* Birch Cabin was going to
copy your costumes? Why would you think
that?"

"Because they copied Jessie's Big Idea,"
Benny blurted out.

Kim seemed to shrink back when Benny
said this.

"Was Me and My Buddy really Jessie's idea, Kim?" Ginny asked.

Kim nodded. "Yes. I couldn't think of anything good for that or for the costumes, either. I'm just good at sports, not the new things you and Rich want us to do. Everything is different from the way Camp Seagull used to be. Lizzie told me about Me and My Buddy, so I raced to your office to make sure I submitted it before Jessie got hers in."

"What about you, Lizzie?" Ginny asked. "Did you have anything to do with that — and with telling Kim about the Dolphins' costumes?"

Lizzie looked like a very unhappy sea turtle. "I did tell Kim about Me and My Buddy so her group would win, not the Aldens'. And I told her about the Dolphins being space aliens, too. But the Aldens fooled everybody."

Jessie looked at Lizzie. "We can't figure out why you don't seem to want us to have a good time at Camp Seagull."

Lizzie stood there, not saying anything. That's when Zach Pines stepped forward from the crowd of campers. "It's not hard to figure out. Lizzie and I were supposed to be overnight campers. Then, at the last minute, Ginny and Rich gave our overnight places to you. My dad's family owned Camp Seagull for a long time, and now Ginny and Rich have taken it over." Zach put his arm around his sister, which wasn't too easy to do because of her turtle shell.

"I was worried I'd never get to be an overnight camper," Lizzie said. "There are four of you and only two of us. So I did things that would make everybody think you shouldn't be counselors. Then maybe you wouldn't be asked back."

"Did you take the flags, too, Lizzie?" Henry asked.

Lizzie looked confused. "The flags? No."

"I did," Zach confessed. "Just for a little while. Then my dad found them in my room at home. He put them back in your cabin yesterday. Flag Ceremony was my favorite job, but then the Gullens gave it to you. My dad and other people in my family always did Flag Ceremony. That's my uncle playing on the bugle tape. I know it doesn't sound as good as Henry's bugle, but it sounds good to us."

Rich walked over to Zach. "I tried to take some responsibility away from you so you could enjoy camp more and not work so hard. I didn't realize I had hurt you. Next year, you can be in charge of Flag Ceremony again."

"We didn't know you were upset about not being overnight campers. We promise we'll make room for you next summer," added Ginny.

"And Zach, I'll teach you how to play the bugle," Henry said. "That reminds me — what about our trunks? Did you leave our trunks behind on purpose the first day? Or was it you, Kim?"

Kim and Zach shook their heads.

"I was so busy, I just forgot them on the beach," Kim said. "I guess I was glad that you would lose points for the Dolphins because you didn't remember to take your trunks. But it wasn't on purpose."

"Same here," Zach confessed. "I saw them on the beach before my dad started the ferry. But I didn't do anything to get them, either. Sorry."

"How about the monster footprints?" Jessie asked.

Lizzie and Kim exchanged looks.

"I did that!" Lizzie said. "It's allowed. Ever since there was a Camp Seagull, we could do pranks to make people scream. You and Rich didn't change that, did you, Ginny?"

"Not really," Ginny answered. "Even when I worked at the camp when I was your age, we had pranks about the monster of Camp Seagull. But not on the first couple of nights. We weren't supposed to scare the new campers until after they were settled in."

"We weren't scared!" the Dolphin girls of Cedar Cabin cried.

"But I am. Some of you are very scary!"

Ginny said, looking around at the sharks, stingrays, and space aliens. "I really don't know which group should take the costume prize."

The score between the Seals and the Dolphins was very close. The Dolphins only needed fifty points to win and the costume contest was worth a hundred points. If Ginny automatically let the Dolphins win because of Kim's poor sportsmanship, that would be unfair to the Seal campers. Ginny turned to Kim, Lizzie, and Zach, and continued, "I don't want the Seals or the Dolphins to be penalized by your actions. But I do think that the three of you owe the camp an apology for your behavior during this Olympics."

The three nodded in agreement.

Benny broke the tension when he piped up, "I've got a good idea. It's not a Big Idea, but a little one 'cause I'm only six."

"What is it?" Rich asked.

"Let the people who are watching us in the audience vote," Benny suggested. "They can write down which team they think has the best costumes. Then we can count up the votes."

Rich and Ginny looked at each other.

"You were wrong, Benny," Rich said. "That is a Big Idea."

After Rich made the announcement about the voting, Ginny handed out slips of paper to the audience. Then Rich sent around some of the campers to collect the votes.

After refreshments, Ginny came out with her soup pot and her serving spoon and banged them together.

"The votes are in! Rich and I will now give the award to the team for the best costumes," she announced.

"Drumroll, please," Rich said.

Ginny banged on the soup pot.

"The Best Costume Award goes to . . . the Dolphins!"

Since Jessie was dressed as a dolphin, she led her group up to the stage. "Thank you," she said to Rich and Ginny when they put a medal around her dolphin neck.

"The Dolphins are also our Olympic

winners!" Ginny announced. "Here's the gold medal."

Jessie pushed Benny forward. "You thought up the costume voting, Benny. You go over and get the medal."

Ginny was careful when she lowered the medal over Benny's head. She didn't want to disturb the cardboard tube he was wearing as part of his whale outfit.

"Let's hear it for the Dolphins!" Rich said.

"Let's hear it for whales, too!" Benny said.

Join the Boxcar Fan Club!

Visit **boxcarchildren.com** and receive a free goodie bag when you sign up. You'll receive occasional newsletters and be eligible to win prizes and more! Sign up today!

Don't Forget!

The Boxcar Children audiobooks are also available! Find them at your local bookstore, or visit **oasisaudio.com** for more information.

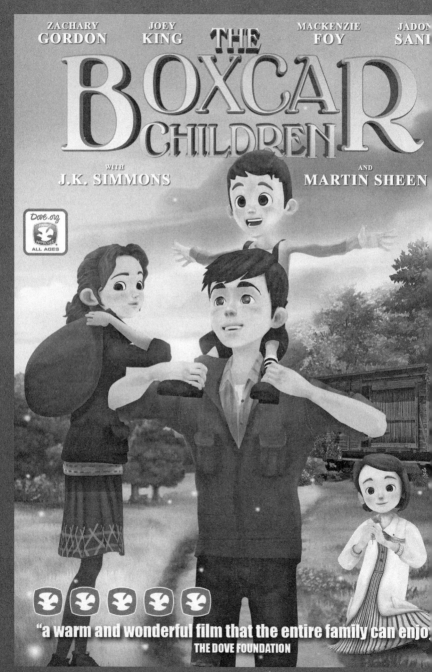

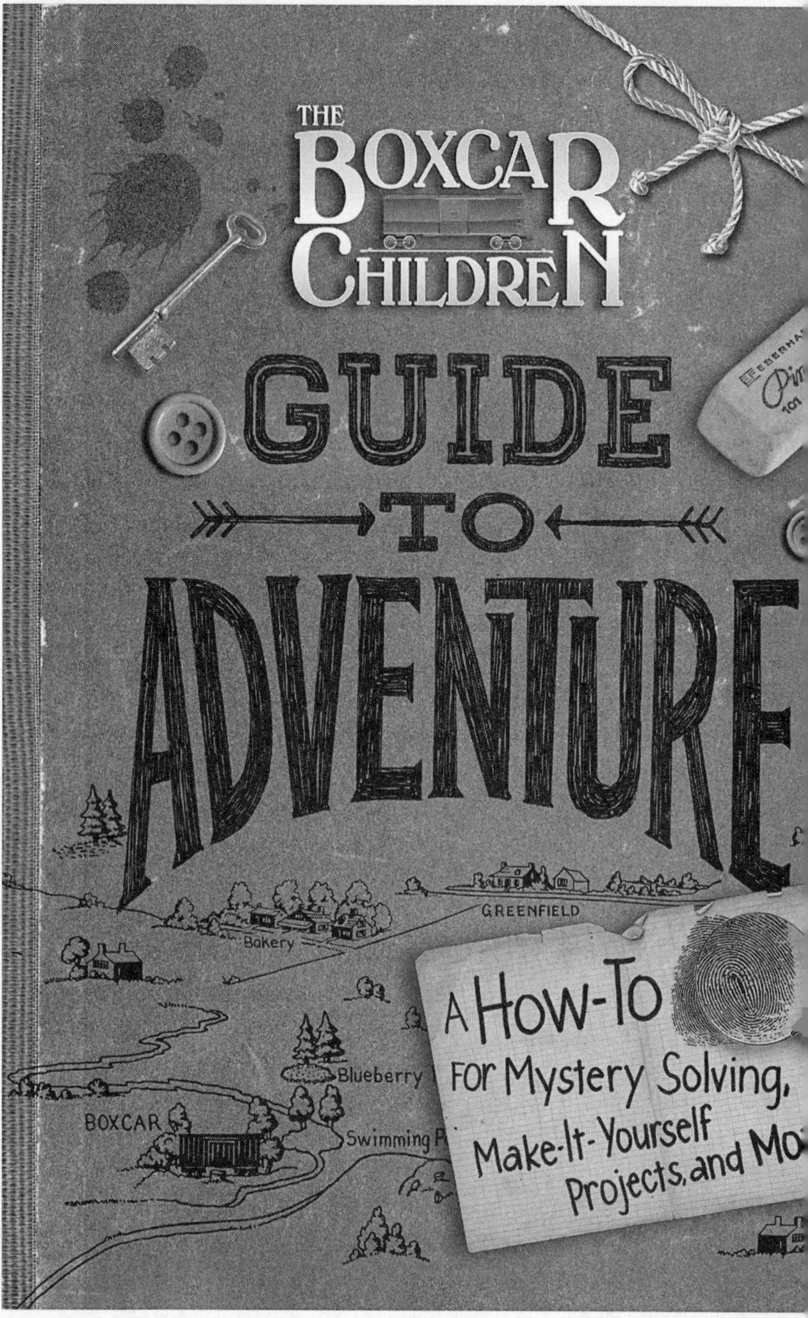

ISBN: 9780807509050,

Create everyday adventures with the Boxcar Children Guide to Adventure!

A fun compendium filled with tips and tricks from the Boxcar Children—from making invisible ink and secret disguises, creating secret codes, and packing a suitcase to taking the perfect photo and enjoying the great outdoors.

PIGPEN CODE

Draw two grids: one like a tic[...] other like a big X. Each letter[...] of the "pen" that it is in.

AB	CD	EF
GH	IJ	KL
MN	OP	QR

When you want to use the[...] letter in the box like a B,[...] place a small dot next to[...]

∙⌐ = B

∨ = T

THE CLUE IN THE D[...]

In *The Mystery of th[...]* photograph with a stra[...] been treated with a spe[...] it into a photography d[...] expose it to light—suc[...]

HOW TO MAKE YOUR OWN MUSTACHE

I **mustache** you a question: [...] the quickest way for a detecti[...] without being noticed? By ch[...] with a snappy mustache! Try [...] brown, red, or black pipe cle[...] upper lip with a piece of tap[...] onto clear tape and stick it [...] mustache shape out of stick[...] backing off the felt and app[...] sly look. For a fluffier must[...] fake fur, then sew elastic o[...] wear securely around your[...]

Mustaches may be dashing[...] be bushy and mysterious. [...] styles to choose from in y[...] mustaches may be used a[...] the curly ones are a dead[...] think you have a caterpil[...]

classic   *caterpillar*   *respectable*

busby   *wiggly*   *funny*

thin   *extravagant*   *downward*

Crack the Code

Mysterious notes are *appearing* and we're ready to solve the mystery. Can you help?

Writing codes, called **cryptography**, has been used for a very long time to send secret messages. Some messages are used to pass **secrets** from one person to another, while other codes are games. Codes may be made up of any symbols such as letters, numbers, or even squiggles. Putting them together forms a code and in order to read it, the other person needs a key to figure it out! **A key** consists of a graph that shows what each symbol represents.

REVERSE ALPHABET CODE

The alphabet code is written with letters in alphabetic order on one line, and the alphabet backward on the next line, so each letter's opposite is directly below it.

```
A B C D E F G H I J K L M N O P Q R S T U V W X Y Z
Z Y X W V U T S R Q P O N M L K J I H G F E D C B A
```

Available wherever books are sold

THE

BOXCAR
CHILDREN

THE LEGEND OF THE IRISH CASTLE

Created by
GERTRUDE CHANDLER WARNER

PB ISBN: 9780807507063, $5.9

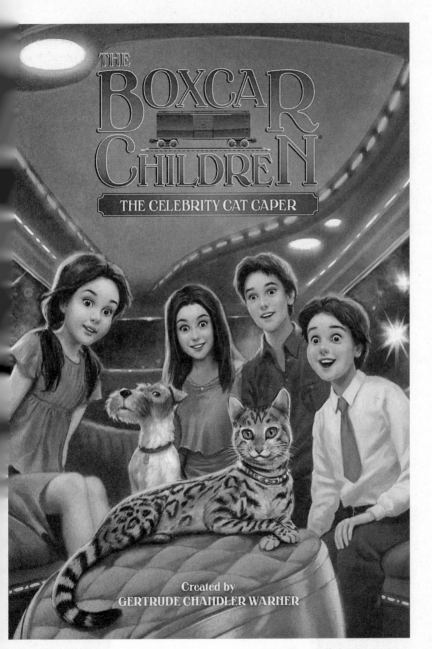

THE BOXCAR CHILDREN

THE CELEBRITY CAT CAPER

Created by
GERTRUDE CHANDLER WARNER

PB ISBN: 9780807507124, $5.99

GERTRUDE CHANDLER WARNER discovered when she was teaching that many readers who like an exciting story could find no books that were both easy and fun to read. She decided to try to meet this need, and her first book, *The Boxcar Children*, quickly proved she had succeeded.

Miss Warner drew on her own experiences to write the mystery. As a child she spent hours watching trains go by on the tracks opposite her family home. She often dreamed about what it would be like to set up housekeeping in a caboose or freight car—the situation the Alden children find themselves in.

While the mystery element is central to each of Miss Warner's books, she never thought of them as strictly juvenile mysteries. She liked to stress the Aldens' independence and resourcefulness and their solid New England devotion to using up and making do. The Aldens go about most of their adventures with as little adult supervision as possible—something else that delights young readers.

Miss Warner lived in Putnam, Connecticut, until her death in 1979. During her lifetime, she received hundreds of letters from girls and boys telling her how much they liked her books.